never

craven

was

the

raven

never

craven

was

the

raven

written and illustrated by michael anthony white

First Printing, 2023

ISBN 978-1-7377921-8-5 (hardcover)
ISBN 978-1-7377921-9-2 (audiobook)

Published by Vox Geekus

for

the players and critics

dreamers

cynics

gamers and geeks and freaks

thinkers

doubters

makers of music

drinkers of mead

THE TOSS OF A WHIMSICAL WRENCH

Writing isn't writ for fun
Too often that I see.
It's rather
Seldom someone shocks me with
A keen capacity
For knowing

That no gates nor boundaries
Must ever be allowed
Within the
Process people pule to be
A mystery in shroud.
This silly

Task of which I'm speaking of
Needs just a bit of guts.
I'll change the
Ruddy regulations and
In turn reverse the ruts
That seem to

Stifle creativity
Thus dampening the fun.
Now let me
Show these shallow shunners just
Exactly how it's done.
Bear witness:

6/16

ORANGE WITH ENVY

All my life they've told me that one cannot rhyme with "orange"

As the concept seems for many a maneuver rather foreign.

Just a pipe dream; wishful thinking from a daydream on the floor when

Germination is in season for the seedling come the morn.

Champagne with apples can be sweet but if you're bothered by the core

A juicy slice or two of citrus can be purchased from the store.

In general, most will try to sell them when you enter through their door

And jams and jellies (when produced with) are delicious! Look out for

Ingesting rind — it may be bitter on your tongue so I implore when

Generating your next meal be sure to peel it. Just a scoring

Gently round the outer edges will then make that rind no more and

Juicy fruit will then be all that's left. *Enjoy* that lovely orange.

YOU'RE THE ONE WITH THE DIRTY MIND

And now I shall tell you a story
(I promise it isn't complex),
Of a gal and a guy who had met on the fly
But don't worry, it's not about

Seconds just after departing
On a joyride she took for a kick,
When passing a tree she was certain to see
A hitchhiker holding his

Thick right-hand thumb out beside him.
It mildly frazzled her wits
Because it was clear that this stranger right here
Was staring at both of her

Tires which suffered a blowout.
Twas obvious things were amiss
For maintenance had been neglected too bad
And now she was taking a

Pitiful spill in a gutter
And her fender got dented a bit.
With growing concern, she had thoroughly learned
Her insurance plan wasn't worth

Shouting for help on her smartphone
To get the car out of the ditch.
She found with a try, a repair shop nearby
And dialed the son of a

Businessman quickly showed up there
And promised to get her unstuck
But it wouldn't have gleamed in her wildest dreams
That he would be such a good

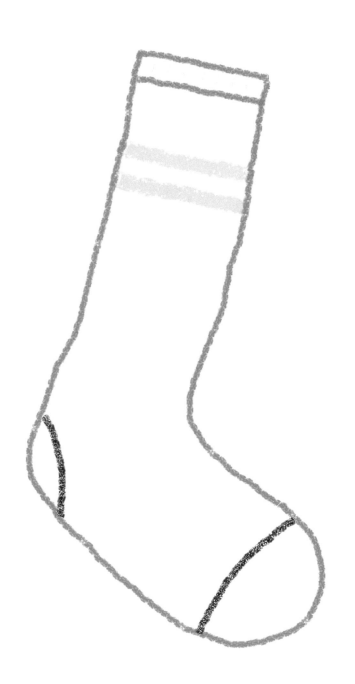

Truck driver from Santa Barbara
Who worked very hard on the clock.
He taught her that dudes who wear big massive shoes
Are likely to have a big

Sock made of thick fluffy fabric
With colors and patterns for flash
Hey, what's with the smirks on your faces you jerks??
Would you get your heads outta the trash?!

RIDICULOUSLY SIMPLE INSTRUCTIONS FOR BREWING ALE

It starts with malted grain found at your local homebrew store.
Some recipes require less and some require more.
You'll steep them in some water at one-fifty Fahrenheit,
But first they must be milled or else it just won't work out right.

An hour to an hour and a half the grain should mash.
Maintain the proper temperature or you'll be left with trash.
When time is up, the sparging of your grain can then begin.
Be gentle, to avoid those bitter tannins deep within.

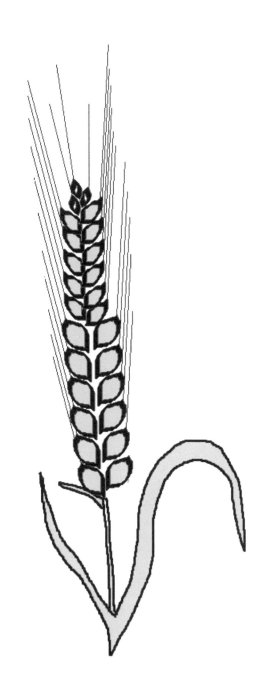

The liquid you are left with is called "wort" (it rhymes with "shirt").
Now bring it to a boil. Do it safely, stay alert.
We do this as to sterilize. It's easy; it's not tough.
A similar duration as the mash should be enough.

Next on the list are pellet hops for flavoring your drink.
Take special care when measuring — they're stronger than you think.
You'll add them when the boil starts, for bitterness and such,
Or toward the end to strengthen the aromas just a touch.

Now go ahead and cool things down to seventy degrees,
Accomplished with an ice bath or a chiller plate for ease.
Within a sanitized container lies the next event:
Combine the lot with brewer's yeast so sugars can ferment.

Provided that your hardware and utensils were all clean,
Lactobacillus cultures won't be entering the scene.
When weeks have passed and ABV has risen to its prime,
You'll sip with joy and realize: Twas surely worth your time!

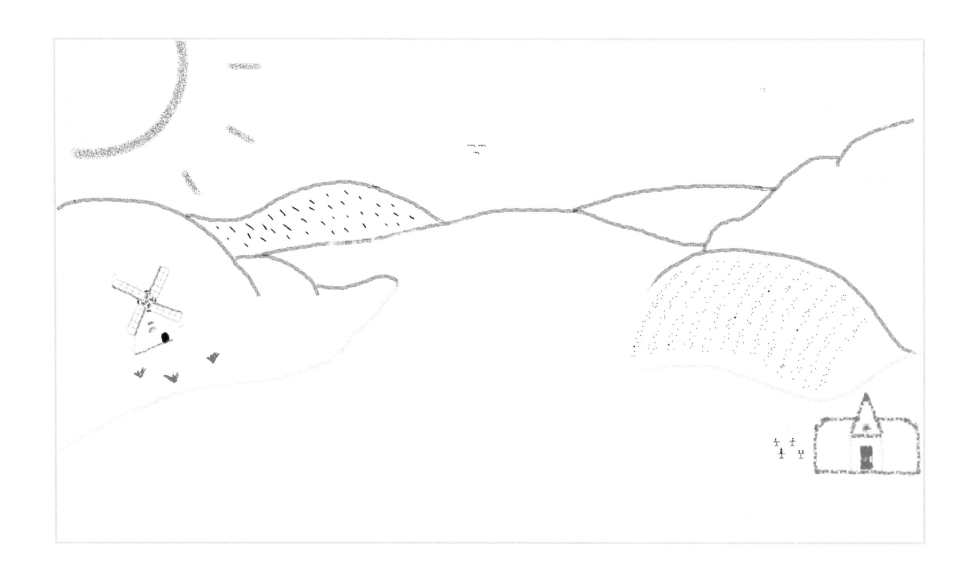

LOCAL LOVE

Living in the valley,
Lots of pastry and cheese.
It could be 20, 50, 80,
Or 100 degrees.
So far away from busy cities
Sitting next to the seas,
We love the wining and the dining
And the delicate breeze.

They're blasting off another rocket
Out at Vandenberg Space.
Subsonic thunder in the morning
Generating some bass.
I'm sure they felt it in Goleta
When it rumbled the place,
But now my wife's awake and has a
Hungry look on her face.

We hear a ruckus in the neighborhood
(The block is awake).
The local BBQ is chopping wood
For smoking a steak.
A few employees in the parking lot
Are taking a break.
My wife and I are looking forward to
The breakfast we'll make.

Sippin' a cup o' the black stuff
(Chicory dash)
Flippin' a couple o' pancakes
(Done in a flash)
Grippin' the maple syrup jug
(Don't let it crash)
Drippin' a drop o' the dark grade
(Personal stash)

A couple relatives are coming
Here to see us today.
So many wineries to visit,
We can see a new play...
Maybe we'll grab an æbleskiver
Or a cafe latte
Before a walk on Copenhagen
To enjoy a sorbet.

Don't forget about the cheese,
The shop'll make you a deal.
You can nibble on a slice
Or you can buy a whole wheel.
Just be sure to save some room
And practice moderate zeal,
'Cause tonight we're going out
For a luxurious meal.

Living in the valley
With the greatest of ease.
It could be 20, 50, 80,
Or 100 degrees.
There's not a worry in the village —
We can do as we please.
We love the wining and the dining
And the delicate breeze.

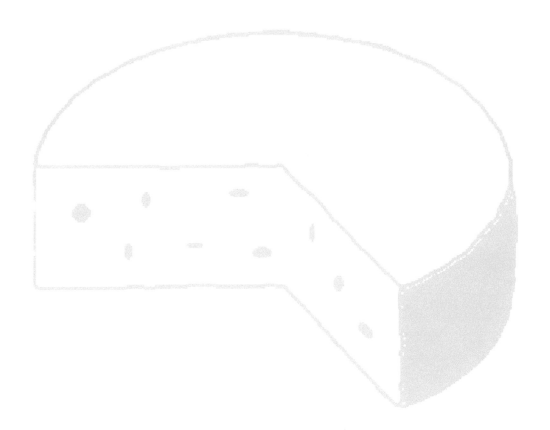

A LOW-BUDGET POEM

The thing about a budget is:
You make it and don't budge.
Not even during harder times
When it becomes a drudge.

Within our own U S of A,
This proud and cherished land,
The average household debt has reached
One hundred fifty grand!

Some people rack up credit cards
From going out to eat,
Or buying things they can't afford
(Although they're pretty neat).

The banks won't be impressed at all
By toys that you have bought
And if you should neglect to pay,
They'll repossess the lot!

In order to achieve complete
Financial harmony,
You'll have to practice discipline —
Willpower is the key.

When comes the time that you've paid off
Your debts in full amounts,
It's clever to establish some
Retirement accounts.

Diversify and choose investments
Wisely and you'll see...
When you've grown old, you'll have become
As comfy as can be.

IN GOOD TASTE

A time long ago in a village most distant,
Once being the newest of residents there,
Some locals had called out to me for attendance:
The neighborhood's very next potluck affair!

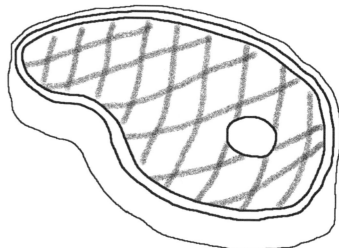

As I'd just arrived in this quaint little haven
So eager to make some new friends in the place
I held many doubts of what I should be bringing
For food and for drink as to not be disgraced.

In hopes of refining my amateur cooking
I figured I'd whip up a favorite fare.
Filet was too pricey for *my* meager budget
Thus, round steak would end up the dish I'd prepare.

Before very long, I discovered a pattern
That seems quite consistent when learning to cook...
Excessive experimentation can leave you
With plates full of nothing but gobbledygook!

I tried many variants, seasonings, spices,
Rehearsing at home a full week with panache.
I tried to take pride in my work so that I could
Ensure a fine dish for the guests at the bash.

By breading and frying each serving so gently
Then ending by baking them slow in a crock,
Aromas were beautiful, textures were tender,
And flavors? Why, *surely* nobody would balk!

When taking to heart all the methods I'd practiced,
These foods I'd prepared without hurry or haste,
I now had acquired this Wisdom as follows:
To learn more of food, one needs merely to taste.

In hopes of expanding my amateur palate
I bought a cheap vessel of wine from a rack
And then chose one more to sip 'longside the first one
With plans of comparing whilst throwing them back.

Surprising to me and despite lower dollar
Amount spent upon the *first* bottle I tried,
Explosions of dark fruit abound had begun to
Burst forth with each droplet I dared to abide.

Yet even additional shockingly humorous
Findings were found of the higher-priced wine:
Sharp notes of hot petrol and mouthfeel of 50-
Grit sandpaper caused me to *strongly* decline!

This effort had clearly revealed unto me that
A price tag does *not* necessarily serve
Indicative of a superior vintage.
Not even when labeled "Estate" or "Reserve."

When taking to heart both the wines that I'd purchased,
These bottles I'd sampled and tried and embraced,
I now had obtained newfound Courage as follows:
To learn more of wine, one needs simply to taste.

Attending the party in stride and good spirit,
Upon the buffet my selections would rest.
One bottle of lesser-priced wine chosen wisely,
One tray of the cuts that I'd given my best.

Some scoffed and avoided the bottle I'd offered,
The label of which was berated and teased.
Some others, however, were happy to try it
And after they sipped, they were pleasantly pleased.

Regarding the steaks I'd prepared with such passion,
One group was *appalled* that "it wasn't filet..."
Refusing to try it, they left it to others
Who loved every bite and proclaimed it gourmet.

These kindhearted guests and I all left that potluck
Soon throwing great parties in homes of our own.
With board games and succulent meals shared aplenty,
Cam'raderie flourished and friendships were grown.

When taking to heart all the people encountered,
These neighborhood folks I had met with and faced,
I now had absorbed a new Powerful lesson:
To make some new friends, one needs only good taste.

FORGOTTEN FUNDAMENTALS

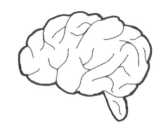

A Basic **C**haracteristic Defends Ethics: Fortitude.

Great Honesty Initiates Justice.

Knowledge, Learned

Mindfully, Nurtures Objectivity.

Pacifying Quarrels Rewards Sincere Treasures...

...Unbridled Vitriol Warrants "**X**" **Y**ielding **Z**ero.

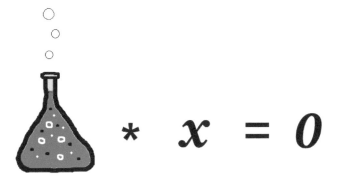 $* \; x \; = \; 0$

ANOTHER CUP?

There's something that has always made
My senses whirl and troubles fade
It feels as if I have a radar for this sacred thing

Come morning after sleeping well
Just as I wake I love to smell
Its roasted rich aroma elegantly traveling

From kitchen to the hall around
The corner where the bedroom's found
I'm guaranteed to soon be bounding up and out of bed

I'll drink it black if I prefer
Or lend a drop of cream and stir
And cappuccino has been *surely* known to clear my head

Robusta or Arabica
Brazilian or from Africa
So long as I can have a cuppa java just for me

It does the trick to caffeinate
Which helps me when I'm working late
Or when my craving won't be sated with a spot of tea.

I slept so terribly last night.
I probably should have brewed a fresh batch before trying to knock this one out.

THAT WRETCHED FOE

You've felt it creep along the weary baseboards of your chest
When in a moment of pure panic, in a bind or under stress.
The unmistakable discomfort never fully rests
Unless it finally gets its way and flaunts a sinister success.

It is a beast that cannot be defeated or disposed
But rest assured a dose of fortitude shall guard you from its throes.
To keep this foul abomination banished and at bay
Requires vigilant persistence lest you then become its prey.

A battle that's as ancient as the oldest speck of dust,
That mortal struggle to defend that which is virtuous and just.
To stand your ground with fervor is the way to guarantee
That wretched foe they call Temptation holds no power over thee.

REBEL B. SPITEFUL

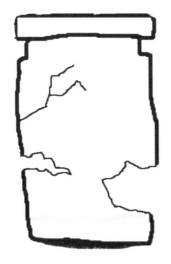

Young Rebel B. Spiteful was spiteful galore
A spitefullest child who cursed and who swore.
"I'll always be spiteful! I'll shout and I'll roar!"

And Rebel B. Spiteful was spiteful once more.

When walking around in a grocery store
This rebel's behavior was one to abhor.
"I love knocking jars off the shelf to the floor!"

And Rebel B. Spiteful was spiteful once more.

One day, nature finally settled the score
When Rebel broke in through a big farmhouse door
And came face to face with a big spiteful boar...

Thus, Rebel B. Spiteful would spite nevermore.

SILLY PEOPLE

I'm often seen laughing and rolling my eyes
At the silly things people around me advise.
I'll share a small dose of what I've heard them say
Since they prob'ly aren't reading these words anyway:

"The bible says, 'Money's the root of all sin!' "
But when I checked the book for the real verse within,
"The love of money..." is the actual quote
(In a letter to Tim, that his buddy Paul wrote).

It isn't semantics, this isn't a game.
I am not splitting hairs, they're not nearly the same.
One blames an inanimate object indeed
While the real lesson teaches to steer clear of greed.

I'm often seen laughing and shaking my head

At the silly things people around me have said.

I hear them at markets, the sidewalks, the street...

Spreading anecdotes they'd heard somebody repeat:

Their claims of big corporations are funny:
"They're not run by people, they're all run by money!"
I wager these folks must all live in a cage.
We don't see eye to eye, we're not on the same page.

I've worked for such places so massive and large
And I've been introduced to the powers in charge.
I've entered their offices — guess what was there?
A flesh and blood human occupying the chair.

My head often spins from below to above

At the silly things people convince themselves of.

If it's within ignorance that they've found bliss,

Then I'm guessing they'd rather not listen to this:

True wisdom cannot be obtained for a fee
And it sure doesn't come from a college degree.
It certainly won't be acquired it seems
Via nourishing bias with internet memes.
Do not presume you'll be respected of course
When refusing to ever consider your source.
To keep up appearances using such fuel...

Isn't just acting silly,

it's being a fool.

STONED

It's been said that one should never leave'm unturned
But it seems in the end I've just been burned
By the stepping stone that once led me to a wondrous land.

Upon clockin' out at the end of the day,
A good time was always just a stone's throw away.
I used ta be so proud to hold a nice cold one in my hand.

No one worried or cared of who wouldn't approve,
All my friends and I would enjoy a stone groove.
Though we didn't get stoned, we'd always take one or two.

But now the stone's started rolling, I've just been told
And I fear in time it might leave us stone cold
So for now — old friend — I'll keep a stony gaze on you.

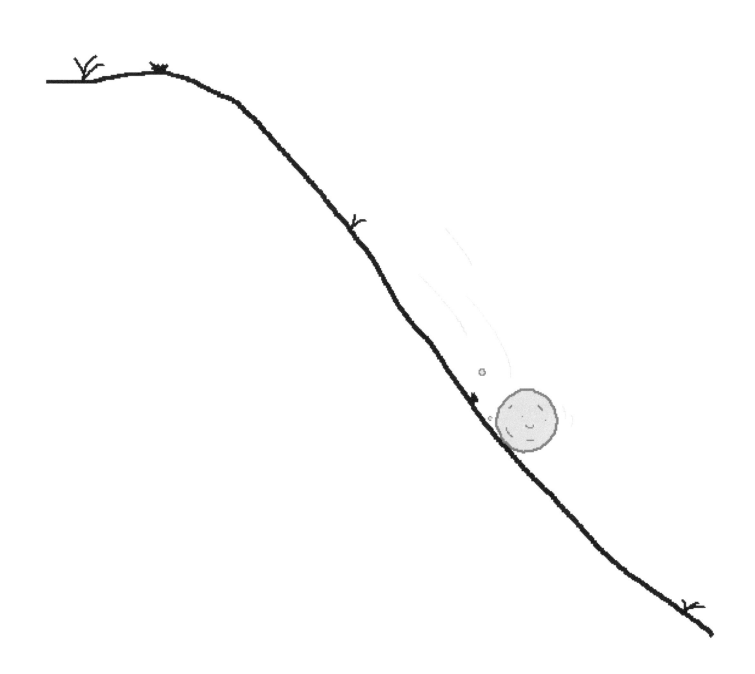

TANGLED IN A WEB

Trendy music to the left
There's a puppy on the right
At the bottom there's a supplement
To help you sleep at night

Just don't bother with the top
'Cause it's looking pretty lame
Stupid kids have found a way to eat
Detergent as a game

 No one said that it would be
Always worthy of your time
Take no guarantees or promises
Be careful it's your dime

Plenty bias to be found
But I guess that all depends
What you're querying and searching for
And how you choose your friends

Don't you blame me how it goes
Expectations have been set
Maybe after all you're not prepared
To browse the internet

MAY

					1	2
3	4	5	6	7	8	9
10	11	12	☠			

730

A seven hundred thirty is a lot to be asked
To ponder and to meditate, compare and contrast.
I've given forth my best as all the days have amassed.
It just so happens seven hundred thirty have passed.

For seven hundred thirty is the start of my day.
Still exercising discipline before any play.
With fortitude and courage, I'll protect what I may
When seven hundred thirty comes to take it away.

Twas seven hundred thirty days ago they would gaffe.
In truth they had mistaken all the wheat for the chaff.
With sights on short-term profits, many had a big laugh
'Til karma came and cut their reputation in half.

A touch of indignation for my wound to be bled
Then onward I did press to face the future ahead.
By cautiously avoiding pity parties of dread
I'm seven hundred thirty times the wiser instead.

A seven hundred thirty is a lot to be asked.
I carry on and calculate, persisting steadfast.
I'm giving forth my best to every day that is cast
For seven hundred thirty shall be far from the last.

THEY

They creep

              They crawl

They
hide
in
the
wall

                                                  They hope that you won't even see them at all

They
p l a n
T h e y   p l o t
They take what they ought
They bring it all back
to the lair they have wrought

They raid

They roam

They pillage and comb

They put you on edge in your very own home

They think   They thrive   They soon will arrive

They evermore do what they must to survive

They quest

They   queue

They now come for you

They know when you're sleeping there's naught you can do

They feel

They find

They play with your mind

They haunt you until you're about to unwind

They ache
They ate
They sampled your bait
They soon will find out you've determined their fate

They're tanks
They're tough
They're rugged and rough
They're biding their time —

they'll be back

soon enough...

DESSERT

Mary and Barry
Were sweet as could be
Mary was merry
Despite her decree
"I'll not abide dairy
Nor lamb fricassee"
Still, Mary and Bar'
Lived harmoniously

Mary and Barry
Soon married, you see
But Bar' had a mare
Of whom did not agree
That Mary would fare
The best pairing for he
So Barry soon buried
That horse by a tree.

When Mary and Barry
Had grown elderly
They made the best fare
Unintentionally
For a hungry black bear
Who was brimming with glee —

It had *always* loved Pie
Made of Marionberry

HIGH STRUNG

I have pity not for the puppet lamenting
The loss of its solace, unable to sleep.

Unlike the fine tale of a puppet by Carlo
So nursing the trace of its soul within deep.

For strings, when not cut shall serve only to nourish
Their masters above who delight in deceit.

With hunger and lust to manipulate others,
No hesitance found in their motives to cheat.

Though trite and still true, this performance continues
Ad nauseam, double-plus-ungood times two.

One question remains for the audience present:
This puppet has never fooled me... has it you?

WRITHE

Have a seat, unlucky winner

Soon you'll be too sore for dinner.

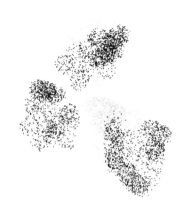

No rejoicing, nothing cheery

Time to pay the piper, dearie.

Yellow lights are strongly glaring

Forming spots out where you're staring

Speaking clearly shan't be netted
Mumbling is all you're letted

Needles sharply penetrating
Streams of blood reciprocating

Eardrums ringing, vision blurring
Sounds of shrill metallic whirring

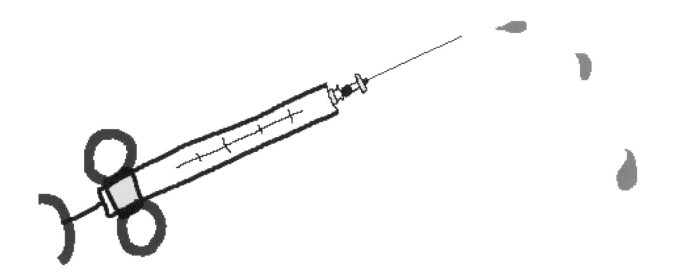

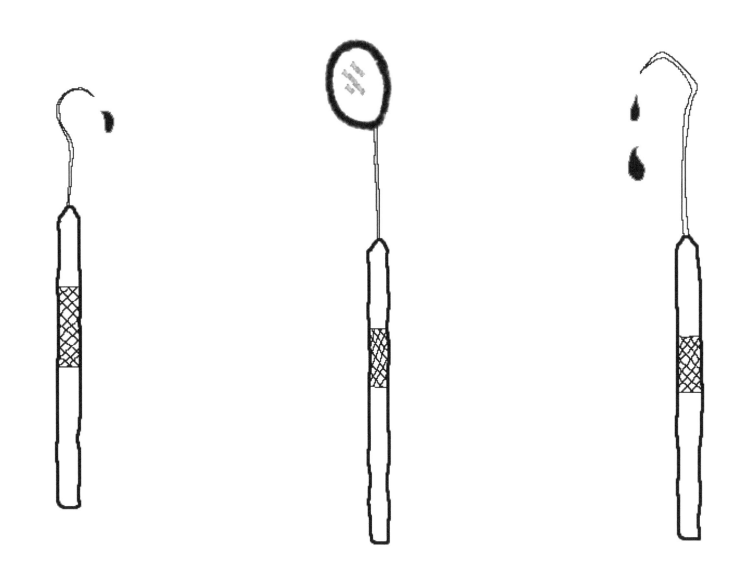

Grinding dentin into powder
Screams of anguish growing louder

Pain was chosen when forgoing
Flossing well, despite your knowing

Hygiene bears no controversy
This chair grants no ounce of mercy.

THE CABARET

Once upon a bleak December, though long past I still remember
Unequivoc'ly the time my peace was tossed unto the fray:
　　Out my door I had departed for a jaunt so quickly started
　　On a course I had not charted, as to melt my stress away.
Little did I know there'd be no chance of melting stress away;
　　　　On my calm, that night would prey.

"Strange," I thought, "...it seems deserted" — when so suddenly alerted
By the lack of other people in the village park that day.
　　On the streets nobody walking, in the taverns no one talking
　　...'Nary but a raven squawking sharply near a small cafe.
So devoid of life but for that bird outside a small cafe,
　　　　Smirking as it flew away.

As I trod in search of solace, darkness cursed the streetlamps' flawless
Glows as time and time again they kept the anxious dusk at bay.
　　Verily I strolled unknowing of an eerie presence flowing
　　Formed of restless souls all growing with intent to have their say.
Oh indeed, how eager were those restless souls to have their say —
　　　　Words that haunt me to this day.

From afar a stranger snickered, as the nearest lamppost flickered
Damaging my calm into a hundred shards of disarray.
Seldom did such harmless token cause my nerve to be so broken
Not a single word was spoken, only laughter heard at play!
As to guess from whom that voice had hailed I did not wish to play,
Yet the game was underway.

Try I did to still my panic; twas no sense becoming manic.
"Take a few deep breaths," I whispered to myself, "You'll be okay.
Yes, perhaps some mild drinking would allay this overthinking,
I can hear the glasses clinking at the pub just down the way!"
Soon I'd find the public house's door to be shut all the way —
It was locked to my dismay.

Striving then to form a theory that could justify these dreary
Actions of dark whimsy that did feast on my naiveté,
    Had it not been long contested: Rancid food left undigested
    Might just leave the wits arrested, causing sense to go astray?
Surely then, a tainted meal had forced my wits to go astray!
        In good time, I'd be okay.

Deep within my skull, a thunder roared as if to tear asunder
Any shred of courage that remained upon my tattered tray.
    Wicked bells reverberating, every wave obliterating.
    None but pain so penetrating, I could not but writhe and pray.
Begging for that agony to cease, how strongly I did pray!
        For how long, I could not say.

Then so quickly as it started, that abomination parted,
Vanishing to leave my senses rattled, stripped, and torn away.
Every nerve completely shaken, confidence was fully taken.
No composure unforsaken as my vision turned to gray.
All the color from the world had faded suddenly to gray,
Now a monochrome display.

With my pulse now elevated, standing very still I waited
For a hint of mercy that would nary be delivered, nay.
Nothing of the sort was granted, nothing but an ill-enchanted
Supernatural wind was planted forcing all to bend and sway.
Buildings, metal, wood, and brick had all been forced to bend and sway,
Wind they could not disobey.

Through the village park I thrusted, 'gainst my will I had been gusted
By that curséd breeze that seemed at last, **at last**, to reach decay.
Suffering with every tumble, wincing through the final stumble
Muttering a painful grumble as my battered body lay.
Gasping for my breath I re'lized where it was that I did lay:
Just outside a cabaret.

Tossed about and slightly nauseous, I arose to sneak a cautious
Glance into the venue so bereft of patrons, bleak and gray:
Bands rehearsing, poets writing, actors, singers, all reciting.
Host and concierge inviting passersby to have a stay.
Ah, but none could see these spectres doomed forever here to stay...
It was but a grim soirée.

"Free us from this cold perdition" begged the emcee apparition
Pleading thus morosely through its moans as best it could convey,
*   "We performers were neglected, overlooked and hence dejected.*
*   Yet our fate may be corrected if successors were to play.*
Bolster our descendants, call their public here to see them play!
*   For your sake, you'll not delay."*

*   With a shriek, the phantoms faded as those colors once degraded*
Made a grand return as there I stood in bright and light of day.
*   In my hand was found a resting leaflet with a phrase requesting.*
*   ('Tis my scruples they were testing — **watching** were those phantoms, they!)*
To you now I read the phrase left with me by those phantoms, they:
*   "go now to the cabaret."*

Michael is a daydreaming introvert from the days of cursive and cassette tapes, raised in the enchanting village of Solvang.

Upon stepping away from the writing desk, he can be found recording music, brewing ale, cider, mead, hosting board game parties, or playing video games with powerfully moving soundtracks.

Always one to share wayward thoughts and uncomfortable perspectives, he's at last fulfilled his desires to chronicle a taste of these haunting reflections for the questionable enjoyment of others.

He still misses Saturday morning cartoons and music videos, dearly.

ALSO AVAILABLE FROM MICHAEL ANTHONY WHITE:

True Tales from the Land of Digital Sand
Essential Information After High School Graduation

voxgeekus.com